MINI CLASSICS

THE

LITTLE
MERMAID

© Parragon Book Service Ltd

This edition printed for:
Shooting Star Press, Inc.
230 Fifth Avenue–Suite 1212,
New York, NY 10001

Shooting Star Press books are available at special
discounts for bulk purchases for sales promotions,
premiums, fund-raising, or educational use. Special
editions or book excerpts can also be created to
specification. For details contact: Special Sales
Director, Shooting Star Press, Inc., 230 Fifth Avenue,
Suite 1212, New York, New York 10001.

ISBN 1 56924 207 0

Printed and bound in Great Britain.

MINI CLASSICS
THE
LITTLE
MERMAID

RETOLD BY STEPHANIE LASLETT
ILLUSTRATED BY ROGER LANGTON

SHOOTING STAR PRESS

F ar out to sea the water is as blue as a cornflower and as clear as the purest crystal, but it is deep. So deep that very, very many church towers could be stacked from the sea-bed, one on top of the other before they would reach the surface high above. Here dwelt the Mer People in their wonderful underwater world and just where the water was deepest stood the palace of the Mer King. It was a magnificent sight with coral walls and amber windows. The roof was made of mussel shells which constantly opened and closed as the sea-water billowed over them.

The Mer King's wife had died some years before so he lived in the palace with his mother and six young daughters. The Princesses were all very beautiful but the youngest was the most beautiful of all. She was a quiet, thoughtful little girl and spent most of her time alone in her garden. Here she planted her

favourite seaweeds in a rainbow of colours. Under the tree was her prize possession, a white marble statue of a boy which she had rescued from a shipwreck.

The fronds of seaweed gently
stroked the cold marble body,
and the little Princess often
sat beside him and wondered
who he might be.

She spent long hours thinking about the upper world and gave her grandmother no peace until the old woman had recounted everything she knew about the human beings who lived in the land above the sea.

"On your fifteenth birthday," said her grandmother, "you will be allowed to rise to the surface. There you can sit on the rocks in the moonlight and watch the ships sail by."

The little girl longed for the years to pass quickly but, alas!

she was the youngest daughter and had to wait six whole years before it was her turn to see the world of men. As each of her sisters came of age and rose to the surface, the little Mermaid would wait eagerly for their news.

Their stories were filled with the sound of ringing church bells, distant music and laughter and far-away bird-song. They saw magical sunsets, dancing dolphins and children playing happily on the shore.

Each sister was quite
enchanted by so many new
delights, but the novelty was
soon over and they were happy
to return to their home deep
at the bottom of the sea.

The youngest Princess was impatient for her time to come.

"If only I was fifteen!" she sighed. "How I wish I could see the upper world!" The years slowly passed and at last her birthday arrived.

"Well, now it is your turn," said her grandmother. "Come, let me dress you," and around the Princess's hair she wound a wreath of white lilies, sprinkled with pearls. The little Mermaid fidgeted and begged her to hurry and at long last she was ready to leave.

"Farewell!" she cried as she rose through the sea like a silver bubble.

When she reached the surface, the sun had just slipped below the horizon and the clouds gleamed pink and gold. The evening star shone in the pale western sky, not a breath of air stirred and the sea was as smooth as a mirror. It was the most beautiful sight she had ever seen. Then, to her delight, she spied a large ship close by.

As the sky above grew dark, hundreds of lamps burst into light, and music and song rang out from the decks. The little Mermaid peeped inside the cabins. There she saw many richly-dressed men but the handsomest of all was a young Prince with large black eyes.

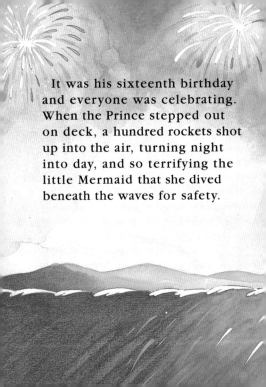

It was his sixteenth birthday and everyone was celebrating. When the Prince stepped out on deck, a hundred rockets shot up into the air, turning night into day, and so terrifying the little Mermaid that she dived beneath the waves for safety.

But soon curiosity got the better of her and up she came again for another look.

The sight that met her startled eyes nearly took her breath away for it seemed as if all the stars of heaven were raining down upon her. Fiery sparks raced across the velvet sky as bright star-bursts exploded high above. All was mirrored in the glassy surface of the water until the light was so great, it seemed like day! The little Mermaid stared and stared.

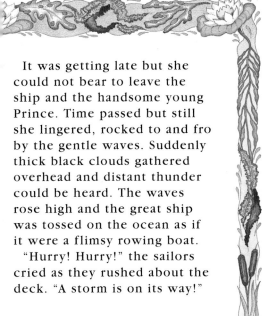

It was getting late but she could not bear to leave the ship and the handsome young Prince. Time passed but still she lingered, rocked to and fro by the gentle waves. Suddenly thick black clouds gathered overhead and distant thunder could be heard. The waves rose high and the great ship was tossed on the ocean as if it were a flimsy rowing boat.

"Hurry! Hurry!" the sailors cried as they rushed about the deck. "A storm is on its way!"

The little Mermaid had never seen such a sight before and did not understand the danger, but the poor crew was terrified and called to God for mercy. Suddenly the ship shuddered, her side cracked and the sea-water poured in. The main mast snapped like a reed and slowly the ship overturned and slid beneath the waves.

Above the howling wind, the little Mermaid could hear the sailors' screams as they clung to the wreckage in the sea.

"The Prince!" she gasped.
"He must not die!" At last she
found him clinging to a broken
beam. His eyes were closed and
he would surely have lost his
grip and drowned had the little
Mermaid not come to his rescue.

With all her strength she held him above the water until morning. Then, when the storm had died down and the sun rose like fire out of the sea, she saw the distant shore and knew she must get him there.

As he lay motionless on the
beam he reminded her of her
own dear statue. Tenderly the
Mermaid kissed his forehead,
stroked the wet hair from his
eyes, then she set out for land,
pulling the Prince beside her.

When she reached the warm
sand she left him and hid behind
the rocks at the water's edge.
There was a school close by
and soon the door opened and
several girls ran down the
steps and across the sand.

Suddenly they stopped. They had discovered the Prince. The Mermaid watched as one girl knelt down by his side whilst her schoolfriends stayed some way off and called to her to come. Their voices roused the Prince and he slowly opened his eyes to see the face of a young girl bending over him.

With a shriek, she jumped to her feet and they all ran back to the safety of their school. Then the Prince remembered a girl rescuing him from the

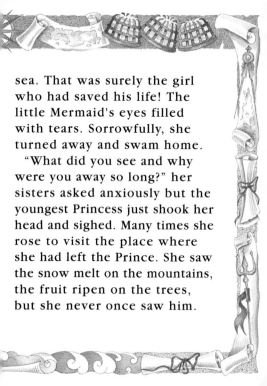

sea. That was surely the girl who had saved his life! The little Mermaid's eyes filled with tears. Sorrowfully, she turned away and swam home.

"What did you see and why were you away so long?" her sisters asked anxiously but the youngest Princess just shook her head and sighed. Many times she rose to visit the place where she had left the Prince. She saw the snow melt on the mountains, the fruit ripen on the trees, but she never once saw him.

Sadly she returned to her marble statue where the seaweeds, now untended, grew wild and free and entwined their long stems and tendrils amongst each other until her whole garden became a bower.

After a time the little Mermaid could bear her unhappiness no longer and with bitter tears recounted her tale to her sisters.

"I only wish I could see him again," she sobbed as she dabbed at her eyes with a soft pink anemone. The Princesses questioned everyone in the Kingdom and at last a young mermaid spoke out.

"I know of this Prince," she said, "and I know exactly where he lives."

"We have found him!" the Princesses told their young sister and soon, arm in arm, all six of them were bobbing in the sea in front of the Prince's Palace. A gold dome crowned the building and inside they could see a tall fountain sparkling diamond-bright.

The moonlight danced on the water and fell on the rich silks and paintings which hung about the rooms. Marble statues stood proudly on guard either side of the white steps which led down to the water.

After that the little Mermaid returned to the Palace almost every day. She watched the young Prince as he sat all alone on the balcony. She listened to the fishermen as they cast their nets and wished that she could speak to them. Humans could sail over the ocean, climb high mountains and walk through green woodlands and how she wished she could, too. One day she visited her grandmother.

"Do humans live forever or do they die like us?" she asked.

"They die as we die," replied the old woman. "And their life is much shorter than ours. We live to the grand age of three hundred years and when we die we become foam on the sea and can never live again. But human beings have souls which continue to live even after their bodies have died."

The Mermaid thought a while. "I wish I could be human, grandmother," she said. "Is there a way that I can live in the upper world and have a soul which will live forever?"

Her grandmother smiled and shook her head.

"Only if you found a man who loved you so deeply that you meant more to him than life itself; who loved you enough to share his whole life with you for all eternity. Then your souls would unite and you would know human bliss. But I am afraid that can never be, little grand-daughter."

"Why, oh why?" begged the little Mermaid.

Her grandmother patted her head. "Because what we see as our most beautiful gift, our tail, is seen by man as something hideous. To be handsome in the upper world, you must have two clumsy stalks, which they call legs."

Sadly the little Mermaid regarded her silvery scales.

"Be happy!" urged the old woman. "You will have three hundred years of joy to fill and then you can rest peacefully when your life is over."

That night there was a Court Ball in the Undersea Kingdom. The crystal clear walls of the ballroom were decorated with hundreds of green and rose-pink shells. From each one a bright light shone forth, streaming across the splendid room and out through the glassy walls, lighting up the ocean.

Hundreds of fish gathered to watch and each one gleamed like a jewel, crimson and purple, silver and gold.

Through the centre of the room flowed a bright, clear stream and there danced the mermen and mermaids.

Sweet song filled the air and
the little Princess sang most
sweetly of all. The Mer People
cheered her and for a moment
she was happy to be reminded
that there was no more lovely
voice than hers in all the sea.
Then her thoughts returned to
the upper world. Sadly, she
remembered her grandmother's
words: 'Three hundred years
of joy.' But the princess felt
her life would never be full of
joy because she could not
forget her handsome Prince.

Quietly she stole away from
the merrymaking and sat alone
in her neglected garden.
"If only I could join my Prince,"
she whispered. Suddenly she
sat up straight. She had
remembered the sea-witch.

"She frightens me dreadfully
but maybe she will know what
to do," said the Mermaid to
herself, and with a determined
toss of her head, she was on
her way. No flowers bloomed
along this path; nothing but
bare, grey sand. Soon she felt
the tug of a frothing, foaming
whirlpool, where the water
whizzed like a mill wheel,
dragging all in its path down
to the abyss below. Strongly
she fought against its steady
pull until she was well clear.

Then she found herself in a boiling, slimy bog and beyond, a wood of trees rose from the ground like hundred-headed serpents. With slimy branches and worm-like fingers, whatever they seized was caught fast forever. Drowned sailors' skulls grinned at her from the murky depths and the little Mermaid's heart pounded with fear.

Fastening up her long waving hair, she swam swifter than a gliding fish, and passed safely through the clutching branches.

51

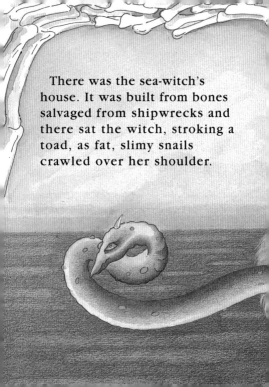

There was the sea-witch's house. It was built from bones salvaged from shipwrecks and there sat the witch, stroking a toad, as fat, slimy snails crawled over her shoulder.

"I know what you want," she said, narrowing her eyes at the little Princess. "Your wish is foolish and bound to bring you unhappiness but it could be granted. You wish to get rid of your tail and grow two stilts to walk upon so that a young Prince may fall in love with you and your soul can live forever — is that not so?"

The witch cackled so wildly that her pet toad and snails fell from her lap. "I will mix you a potion and when you swallow it your tail will shrink away to form those things which men call legs. It will be very painful and every step will feel as though you walk on sharp knives. Can you endure all this suffering?"

"Yes, I will do it," answered the Princess in a trembling voice, as she thought of her dear Prince and their life together.

"But remember," said the sea-witch. "Never again will you be a mermaid and you may never return to your home."

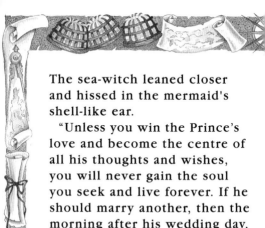

The sea-witch leaned closer
and hissed in the mermaid's
shell-like ear.

"Unless you win the Prince's
love and become the centre of
all his thoughts and wishes,
you will never gain the soul
you seek and live forever. If he
should marry another, then the
morning after his wedding day,
your heart will break with
sorrow, and you will die and
become foam on the sea."

"Still I am willing," said the
little Mermaid, pale as death.

"Then you must pay me for my trouble," hissed the witch. "And it is no small thing that I ask. You have the sweetest voice in all the sea — you must give it to me!"

"But if you take my voice," said the Princess, "what shall I use to charm the Prince?"

"Your grace and beauty," replied the witch, "and your eloquent eyes. With gifts like these it will be easy to win his heart."

"Let it be so," whispered the Princess and so the witch began.

The old sea-witch scooped up a handful of snails.

"Cleanliness is important," she remarked cheerfully as she scrubbed the inside of her big black cauldron with the poor little creatures.

Then the sea-witch scratched
her bosom and let the black
blood trickle down into her
cauldron. She added bladder-
wrack, spume and other
strange ingredients until
smoke rose from the mixture
and formed horrible shapes
above the pot. At last the
magic drink was ready.

"Here it is!" cried the Witch,
handing her a bottle and before
the Mermaid had time to think,
the old crone leant over and
cut her tongue from her head.

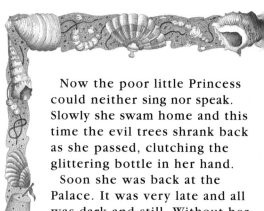

Now the poor little Princess could neither sing nor speak. Slowly she swam home and this time the evil trees shrank back as she passed, clutching the glittering bottle in her hand.

Soon she was back at the Palace. It was very late and all was dark and still. Without her tongue the Mermaid could not bid her family farewell and her heart felt ready to break.

Waving goodbye again and again, she rose through the dark blue waters to the world above

and left her home forever.

The sun had not yet risen when she arrived at the Prince's Palace. Wearily she pulled herself up onto the marble steps and, with one swallow, she drank the strange potion. It ran through her body like a sharp knife and, with a cry, the Mermaid fell down in a dead faint. When she awoke she saw beside her the handsome young Prince with the coal-black eyes.

"Who are you?" he asked.

But the poor Mermaid could
only smile in reply, for, alas! she
could not speak. Gently the
Prince offered her his hand and
led her into the Palace. Then
the sea-witch's prediction came
true for every footstep felt like
a knife-cut, but the Princess
bore the pain bravely.

All who saw her marvelled at
her beauty for she was lovelier
than any girl ever seen before.
The royal maids dressed her in
clothes of muslin and soft silk
and bade her rest a while.

Sweet music drifted into the
room and the little Princess arose.
Down the stairs she went and,
stretching out her delicate
white arms, she danced lightly
about the room until all were
captivated by her grace. The
young Prince was enchanted so
she danced for him again, even
though every step was agony.

From that day on she spent all her time in the Prince's company. They rode on horse back through the green woods and climbed steep mountains until her poor feet bled. But still she smiled and her good, sweet nature charmed all who met her. Every night she would descend the marble steps and soothe her burning feet in the cool sea water, and then she would think of her beloved family down below. One night she could hear her sisters sadly singing and called to them. They were overjoyed to find her and told her of their father's misery at losing his youngest daughter. But the little Mermaid could only weep in reply and, with a final wave, they sank once more below the surface of the sea.

The little Mermaiden became more and more dear to the Prince as the days went by, but he looked upon her as a sweet, gentle child and the thought of making her his wife never entered his head.

The little Mermaid longed for him to prove his affection.

"Do you not love me above all the others?" her eyes seemed to ask, as he held her fondly in his arms.

"You are dearer to me than any other, for no-one is as honest and true as you!"the Prince would say. "You remind me of a girl whom I saw just once and may never see again. She tended me as I lay lifeless on the sand and I can never forget her."

"Alas! He does not know that it was I who saved his life," sighed the little Mermaid.

Time passed and the King and Queen decided that the Prince should marry the daughter of a neighbouring king. The little Mermaid was frantic with fear. "Now my Prince will never marry me and I will never win my soul!" she thought. But the Prince was not happy with the plan either.

"I must obey my parents and visit this Princess," he told her, as he tenderly stroked her hair, "but they cannot force me to marry her. And it is quite impossible for me to love her for she will not be like the beautiful girl who saved me from the sea."

The next day they set out on
board the Royal Ship. Across
the sea they sailed and as the
ship approached the King's
splendid capital, loud trumpets
heralded their arrival.

Bright banners welcomed
them ashore. There waited the
Royal Party and the little
Mermaid's heart missed a beat,
for the Princess was beautiful
and she knew the Prince would
be sure to fall in love.

Sure enough, the Prince clapped his hands with joy.

"It is her!" he cried. "She is the one who saved my life when I lay like a corpse on the seashore." The Princess was indeed the very same girl who had found him lying close to death — but she was not the one who had saved him. The Prince turned to the little Mermaid.

"Be thankful for me, little one. You love me more than any other and must surely wish me to find true happiness?"

But the little Mermaid kissed his hand in silent sorrow and it seemed to her as if her heart was breaking already. Now she knew that she had lost both this world and the next. She would never live forever.

The Princess was equally well pleased with the Prince and so the wedding was agreed upon. As the church bells rang merrily, the bride and bridegroom held hands while the priest read the words which united them.

The little Mermaid stood
behind the Princess and held
the train of her bridal dress.
But she heard not the stirring
music, nor saw the solemn
majesty of the holy ceremony.

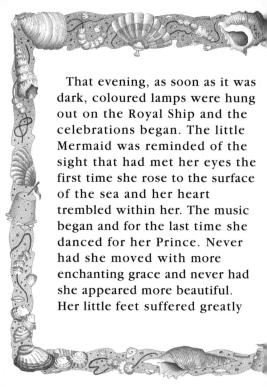

That evening, as soon as it was dark, coloured lamps were hung out on the Royal Ship and the celebrations began. The little Mermaid was reminded of the sight that had met her eyes the first time she rose to the surface of the sea and her heart trembled within her. The music began and for the last time she danced for her Prince. Never had she moved with more enchanting grace and never had she appeared more beautiful. Her little feet suffered greatly

but she no longer felt the pain.
She had forsaken her home
and family. She had given away
her beautiful voice. She had
exhanged her silver tail for
agonising footsteps— all for her
Prince, and all without his
knowing that she was the one
who had saved him from the
storm.

The party ended and the ship
was now still. All alone, the
little Mermaid leaned on the rail
and looked eastwards, waiting
for the dawn.

All at once she saw her sisters rise from the sea. Their faces were deadly pale and their beautiful long hair no longer fluttered about their shoulders for it had all been cut off.

"We have given it to the sea-witch," they called. "She demanded it when we begged her to help you. She has given us a knife and with this you can be saved!. Before the sun rises, you must plunge it into the Prince's heart and when his warm blood trickles down upon your feet, they will be changed back into a fish's tail. Once more you will be a mermaid — but hurry! The sun is rising in the eastern sky and soon it will be too late!

The unhappy Mermaid took the knife and, creeping inside, drew aside the curtains of the bridal bed. Slowly she kissed the forehead of the sleeping Prince and the deadly knife trembled in her hand.

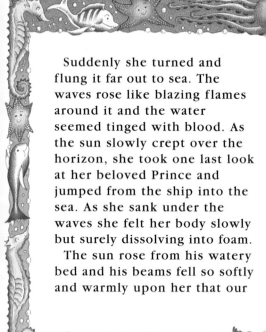

Suddenly she turned and flung it far out to sea. The waves rose like blazing flames around it and the water seemed tinged with blood. As the sun slowly crept over the horizon, she took one last look at her beloved Prince and jumped from the ship into the sea. As she sank under the waves she felt her body slowly but surely dissolving into foam.

The sun rose from his watery bed and his beams fell so softly and warmly upon her that our little Mermaid was scarcely aware she was dying. Over her head hovered a thousand beautiful spirits singing with sweet voices. Then the little Mermaid saw that she had a body as transparent as theirs and she felt herself raised up from the foam.

"We are the daughters of the air," they softly said, as they floated around her. "We do not need the love of man to live forever. We win everlasting life by doing good and kind deeds.

We fly to hot countries where
children breathe bad air and
waste away. We bring our
cooling breath and revive
them. We carry sweet flower
fragrances wherever we go

and spread health and delight
over all the earth. By doing
good in this manner for three
hundred years, we win eternal
life. Now you are one of us
and may also win your soul."

The little Mermaid stretched out her gossamer arms to the sun and tears filled her eyes. Down below she could see the Prince with his pretty bride and knew that they would miss her. Suddenly the Mermaid realised she was no longer unhappy. Unseen, she smiled upon them and wished them great happiness, then joining the children of the air, she lifted her face and soared high above the rosy clouds.

HANS CHRISTIAN ANDERSEN

Hans Christian Andersen was born
in Odense, Denmark, on April 2nd, 1805.
His family was very poor and throughout
his life he suffered much unhappiness.
Even after he had found success as a
writer, Hans Christian Andersen felt
something of an outsider, an aspect which
often emerged in his stories and can be
seen clearly here in the character of
the little Mermaid.
His fairy stories, famous throughout
the world, include *The Snow Queen*,
The Ugly Duckling and *The Emperor's
New Clothes*, and are amongst the
most frequently translated works
of literature.